REBECCA OF SUNNYBROOK FARM

REBECCA
OF SUNNYBROOK FARM

Kate Douglas Wiggin

Retold by
Don Hinkle

Illustrated by
Peter Elwell

Troll Associates

Library of Congress Cataloging in Publication Data

Hinkle, Don.
  Rebecca of Sunnybrook Farm.

    Summary: Talkative, ten-year-old Rebecca goes to
live with her spinster aunts, one harsh and demanding,
the other soft and sentimental, with whom she spends
seven difficult but rewarding years growing up.
  [1. Aunts—Fiction. 2. New England—Fiction]
I. Elwell, Peter, ill. II. Wiggin, Kate Douglas Smith,
1856-1923. Rebecca of Sunnybrook Farm. III. Title.
PZ7.W638Re   1988   [Fic]   87-15475
ISBN 0-8167-1217-4 (lib. bdg.)
ISBN 0-8167-1218-2 (pbk.)

Every day, Mr. Jeremiah Cobb drove the stagecoach through the dusty roads and small towns in Maine. As he pulled the stagecoach into Maplewood, a young girl was already waiting to board. Her name was Rebecca Rowena Randall. She would be the only passenger this day. Her mother, Aurelia, helped Rebecca into the stagecoach. Then Mrs. Randall put a bouquet of flowers beside her daughter and paid the fare.

Mrs. Randall spoke to the driver. "I want you to take Rebecca to my sisters in Riverboro. Do you happen to know Miranda and Jane Sawyer?"

"Well, bless my soul," said Mr. Cobb. "Indeed I know them. They live in a large brick house there."

Nodding, Mrs. Randall looked at her daughter. "Good-bye, Rebecca. Don't get into mischief. And sit still, so you'll look neat and nice when you get there."

"Good-bye, Mother. Now don't worry. Remember, I've traveled before."

Mrs. Randall laughed. "That wasn't traveling, Rebecca," she said. In all of her life, Rebecca had not gone farther than two miles from their farm. The exception was one overnight visit last year to her relatives.

"It *was* traveling, Mother," the girl insisted. "We put lunch in a basket, left the farm, and went on the train. And we carried our nightgowns."

Shocked, Mrs. Randall whispered, "You shouldn't talk about nightgowns in a tone of voice that can be overheard."

"I know, Mother, I know. All I wanted to say was —"

At that moment, Rebecca was thrown back against her seat, as Mr. Cobb slapped the reins and the horses lurched forward. Unruffled, she moved to the window again.

"All I wanted to say was that it *is* a journey when —"

This time, her voice was muffled by the galloping hooves of the horses. They pulled the stagecoach away quickly. Rebecca had to put her head out the window so her mother could hear her.

"It *is* a journey when you carry a nightgown!" shouted Rebecca over the noise, waving to her mother.

Mrs. Randall waved back and sighed. I guess my sisters will have their hands full with Rebecca, she thought. But maybe it will help her ... and them.

The stagecoach traveled along the road to Riverboro. The day grew warmer, though it was still only the middle of May. Mr. Cobb held the reins loosely as he leaned back in his seat atop the stagecoach.

Inside, however, Rebecca was uncomfortable. Her calico dress had been starched so stiffly that it caused her to slide sideways on the leather cushions. She braced her feet against the opposite seat and extended her hands on each side to keep herself in one place. But each time the wheels sank into a rut or jolted suddenly over a stone, she bounced into the air. Finally, she pushed back her straw hat and picked up her pink parasol. Then she looked into her beaded purse to make sure that the few coins there had not been lost.

The sun was making Mr. Cobb sleepy. Suddenly he heard a small voice above the rattle of the stagecoach. He turned and saw his lone passenger leaning out the window. A long black braid of hair swung with the motion of the stagecoach. Rebecca was holding her hat in one hand and with the other was trying to prod the driver with her little pink parasol.

Mr. Cobb stopped the horses.

"Does it cost any more to ride up there with you?" Rebecca asked. "I've slid around down here so much that I'm almost black and blue. Besides, I can't see anything."

Mr. Cobb thought for a moment, then said, "No, it doesn't cost any extra." He got out of his seat to help her out of the coach. Then he helped her up to the front seat.

Rebecca carefully smoothed her dress under her and put her parasol beside her. "Oh, this is better!" she said delighted. "*This* is traveling! I'm a real passenger now."

Mr. Cobb asked, "Why don't you put up your parasol?"

"Oh, dear, no!" answered Rebecca. "I never put it up when the sun shines. Pink fades, you know, and I only carry it to church on cloudy Sundays. It's the dearest thing in life to me, but it's a big responsibility."

Jeremiah Cobb pushed his hat back and took his first good look at the passenger. Rebecca stared back with friendly curiosity. Mr. Cobb noticed that her calico dress was faded, but clean and starched. Her slender throat was very tanned and thin. Her head looked too small to hold up the long thick braid of dark hair hanging down to her waist. But Mr. Cobb thought her eyes were the most interesting he had ever seen. Rebecca's eyes glowed like two dancing stars.

"A lady gave me the parasol," said Rebecca. "Did you notice the pink double ruffle? And the white tip and handle are ivory. The handle is scratched now. See? That's because Fanny sucked and chewed it when I wasn't looking."

"Who's Fanny? Your dog?"

"She's one of my sisters, of course."

"Well, how many of you are there?"

"Apart from mother, seven. Let's see. Hannah Lucy is the oldest. Then I come next. Then there are John Halifax, Jenny Lind, Marquis, Fanny Ellsler, and Miranda, who is named for our aunt, Miranda Sawyer. But we call her Mira. She's three years old. She was born the day Father died."

"Well, that's a big family."

"Far too big. Everybody says that," said Rebecca with a sigh. "They're dear, but such a bother and cost to feed! Hannah and I haven't done anything but put babies to bed at night and take them up in the morning. We've done this for years and years. Mother has her hands full with the cooking and the farming."

"Oh, you live on a farm, do you? Where is that?"

"Our farm is far off from nearly everywhere, but our school and church are at Temperance. That's only two miles." Rebecca smiled prettily and looked around at the country-side as the coach moved along. "Sitting up here with you is almost as good as climbing the church steeple. I know a boy who did that—climbed the steeple. He said the people and cows looked as small as flies!"

Rebecca let out a slow breath. "I'm kind of disappointed because the cows don't look as little from here as I hoped they would." She paused, then brightened. "Still, they don't look as big as if we were on the ground, do they?" Rebecca rushed the conversation along without giving Mr. Cobb a chance to understand.

Finally he broke in. "Your mother's farm," he said. "That isn't the old Hobbs place, is it?"

"No, it's just Randall's farm. That's what Mother calls it. I call it Sunnybrook Farm."

Mr. Cobb didn't like problems, so he shrugged. "I guess it doesn't make any difference what you call it."

Rebecca looked very serious when she turned to him. "Oh, don't say that! It *does* make a difference what you call things! When I say 'Randall's farm,' can't you hear how plain it sounds?"

"No, can't say I do," responded Mr. Cobb uneasily.

"Now, when I say 'Sunnybrook Farm,' what does that make you think of?"

Mr. Cobb looked worried as he tried to figure out an answer to her question. Finally he said, "I suppose there's a brook somewhere near it."

Rebecca looked a little disappointed. "That's pretty good," she said, trying to be encouraging. "There *is* a brook, but not just any old brook. It has young trees and baby bushes on each side of it, and it's a shallow, chattering little brook with a white, sandy bottom and lots of small, twinkling pebbles. Whenever the sun shines, it's full of sparkles all day long."

Mr. Cobb nodded. "Oh, I see," he said.

Rebecca looked around and then sighed. "I'm so hungry, my stomach feels hollow!"

"You better eat your lunch, then. We won't get to your aunts' house for another couple of hours. I never eat until I get to Milltown. So go ahead with your lunch if you want."

Rebecca clasped her hands and said enthusiastically, "Oh, I wish I could see Milltown! I suppose it's big and grand—like Paris. The lady who bought my pink parasol told me about Paris."

"Paris isn't so great," said Mr. Cobb matter-of-factly. "It's one of the dullest places in Maine."

"No, not Paris, Maine," said Rebecca. "I'm talking about

Paris, France. You have to go to it on a boat. It's in my geography book."

They chatted pleasantly for the next few hours, so it was a gentle surprise to both when Mr. Cobb heard himself say, "This is the last long hill. When we get to the top of it, we'll see the chimneys of Riverboro in the distance. It isn't far. I live about half a mile beyond the brick house myself."

"I didn't think I was going to be afraid, but I guess I am just a little bit," said Rebecca.

"Want to go back home?"

"I may be frightened, but I'd be ashamed to run. Going to Aunt Miranda's is like going down to the cellar in the dark. There might be ogres and giants under the stairs—but there *might* be elves and fairies and enchanted frogs! Is there a main street in the village?"

"I suppose you might call it a 'main street,' and your aunts live on it. But there are no stores."

She sighed. "It would be so thrilling to drive down a real main street, sitting high up here behind two splendid horses, with my pink parasol up and everybody in town watching."

Mr. Cobb coughed politely and said, "I guess there isn't any harm in our making a grand entrance in the best style we can. I'll take the whip out and drive fast. Hold your bouquet in your lap, open your little parasol, and we'll make them take notice!"

Excitement ran through Rebecca's body. Her face glowed for a moment, but the glow faded just as quickly. "I forgot—Mother put me inside the stagecoach and maybe she'd want me to be inside when I got to Aunt Miranda's. Then I could open the door and step down like a lady. Would you please stop a minute, Mr. Cobb, and let me sit inside?"

The switch was made. And as the stagecoach rumbled down the street, people peering out their windows could see a proud girl with a bouquet and a parasol in the back seat.

13

The stagecoach stopped at the side door of the brick house, and Mr. Cobb helped Rebecca out like a real lady passenger. The two maiden aunts were already waiting for her. Both seemed cold and distant, though Aunt Jane gave a somewhat warmer kiss of welcome to Rebecca than did Aunt Miranda. Rebecca put the bunch of faded flowers in Aunt Miranda's hand.

"You needn't have bothered to bring flowers," Miranda said. "Our garden's always full of them here."

Mr. Cobb coughed and said, "Well, Miranda and Jane, you've got a lively little girl there." He tipped his hat and drove off.

Miranda Sawyer shuddered at the word "lively." It was a strong belief of hers that children should be seen and not heard. She promptly marched Rebecca into the house.

14

"I'll take you upstairs now and show you your room, Rebecca," Aunt Miranda declared. She was already halfway up the stairs. "Shut the screen door tightly behind you to keep the flies out. It isn't fly time yet, but I want you to start off on the right foot. Wipe your feet well on that braided rug. Hang your hat and cape in the entryway as you go past. Always remember to go up the back way—we don't use the front stairs. We must protect the carpet." They were both on the second-floor landing now. "This is your room on the right here. Go on in! When you've washed your face and hands and brushed your hair, you can come down. We'll unpack your bags later. I say, haven't you got your dress on backwards?"

Rebecca lowered her chin and looked at the row of buttons running up and down directly below it.

"Well, if you have seven children, you can't keep buttoning and unbuttoning them all the time—they have to do it themselves. We're always buttoned up in front at our house."

Miranda raised her eyes skyward, sighed, and closed the door, leaving Rebecca alone in her room.

On the following Monday, Rebecca began her education at a little schoolhouse on the crest of a hill. The teacher, Miss Dearborn, was only eighteen, and this was her first year of teaching. Among Rebecca's classmates was Emma Jane Perkins, the shy daughter of a well-off blacksmith. She soon grew to adore Rebecca. Also in the class were the Simpson children. They weren't well-off at all, and their father often found himself in jail for borrowing from neighbors without first asking.

Rebecca felt lucky to have her books and her new classmates during her first summer in Riverboro. The brick house felt cold and dark to her, and when she wasn't doing schoolwork, she had to keep busy at household tasks.

She wasn't permitted to play outdoors except for an hour on Saturday and Sunday afternoon. In trying to please Aunt Miranda, Rebecca only irritated her with everything she did or didn't do. She continually forgot about going up the back way and would start up the front stairs instead because it was the fastest way to her bedroom. She was willing to go on errands but often forgot what she was sent for. She left the screen door open, letting in the flies. She sang or whistled when she was working. She was always picking flowers—putting them in vases, pinning them on her dress, and sticking them in her hat.

To Aunt Miranda, Rebecca seemed to be an everlasting reminder of the child's dead father, foolish and worthless. Miranda felt his handsome face and charming manners had deceived her sister Aurelia. She was convinced that the only way to save Rebecca from being like her father was to keep her busy constantly and to be very strict with her.

Compared to Aunt Miranda, however, Aunt Jane was like sunshine in a dark place for Rebecca. She came to depend on Aunt Jane's understanding eyes and soft voice.

There were no secrets in the villages that lay along the banks of the river. And there was plenty of spare time to talk about them—under the trees in the hayfield at noon, on the bridge at nightfall, or seated near a stove in the village store during the evening. The neighbors knew that Rebecca and her aunt Miranda were not getting along in that brick house. And most of the neighbors felt sympathy for Rebecca.

Friday afternoon was always the time for songs, poems, and recitations at school. But it was not a happy time. The children disliked memorizing and dreaded getting up in front of their classmates and forgetting their lines. This possibility of failure brought an air of gloom and anxiety to every Friday.

Rebecca was the exception. She decided to put a new spirit into Friday afternoon at the schoolhouse. She taught Elijah and Elisha Simpson to recite three verses of a song with delightful comic effect and gave Susan Simpson a humorous poem to recite. Emma Jane Perkins and Rebecca made up a skit together about a city girl (Rebecca) and a country girl (Emma Jane). Being with Rebecca gave Emma Jane more confidence than she had ever known.

One Friday morning, Miss Dearborn announced that she had invited the doctor's wife, the minister's wife, two members of the school committee, and a few mothers to visit. She asked Rebecca to decorate one of the blackboards for this special occasion. Before the eyes of the class, she drew an American flag with red, white, and blue chalk. Every star was in its right place, and every stripe seemed to flutter as if in a breeze.

All of her classmates clapped loudly. Rebecca's heart leaped for joy, and she felt tears rising in her eyes. She could hardly see the way back to her seat. Never before had she been singled out for applause.

Miss Dearborn dismissed the morning session at quarter to twelve so the pupils could go home for a change of dress. "Will your Aunt Miranda let you wear your best pink dress to play the city girl again?" asked Emma Jane.

"Oh, dear! I better ask Aunt Jane," Rebecca decided.

But she found her lunch on the table and a note saying that both of her aunts had gone visiting. Could she—dare she—wear the pink gingham dress without asking?

I'll wear it, thought Rebecca. They're not here to ask, and maybe they wouldn't mind a bit.

The afternoon was one triumph after another for the children. There were no failures and no tears. Miss Dearborn received many compliments from her invited guests, but she wondered whether they belonged to her or to Rebecca.

As for Rebecca, she floated home, lifted in spirits by the whole afternoon. When she entered the side yard, though, she saw Aunt Miranda waiting for her in the open doorway. Her aunt was clearly angry.

"Who gave you permission to wear that good new dress on a school day?" Her eyes flashed fire.

"I intended to ask you, Aunt Miranda, but you weren't at home. So I couldn't."

"You did no such thing. You put it on because you *knew* I wouldn't have let you."

The happiness Rebecca felt earlier was gone. "But I thought you *would* have given your permission if you had known it was an exhibition at school."

"Exhibition!" exclaimed Miranda scornfully. "Were you exhibiting your parasol?"

"I guess I didn't need to take the parasol," admitted Rebecca, hanging her head. "Emma Jane and I did a skit about a city girl and a country girl, and I was the city girl. I had to dress the part. I haven't hurt the dress any, Aunt Miranda."

"It's your sly, underhanded ways I object to. You went up the front stairs to your room, but you didn't hide your tracks. You dropped your handkerchief on the way. You never cleared away your lunch nor set away a dish. And you left the side door unlocked so anybody could come in and steal what they liked!"

Rebecca slumped down in a chair. Tears began rolling down her cheeks. Miranda didn't care. "It's no good crying over spilled milk. An ounce of good behavior is worth a pound of repentance. Instead of trying to make as little trouble as you could in a house that isn't your own home, you obviously have tried to see how much you could put us out. I have no patience at all for your flowers and frizzed-out hair and airs and graces." Miranda was sneering now. "For all the world, you're just like your good-for-nothing father."

Rebecca lifted her head in a flash. "Look here, Aunt Miranda, I'll be as good as I know how to be. I'll do what I'm told to do, and I'll take my scoldings when I'm bad. But I *won't* have my father called names. He was a perfectly lovely father, and it's very *mean* of you to call him good-for-nothing!"

"Don't you *dare* talk back to me in that impudent way, young lady! Your father was a vain, foolish, shiftless man. You might as well hear it from me as anybody else. He spent all of your mother's money and left her with seven children to provide for."

"At least it's something to leave seven nice children," said Rebecca sobbing.

"Not when other folks have to help feed, clothe, and educate them," responded Miranda coldly. "Now you step upstairs, put on your nightgown, and go to bed and stay there till morning."

Rebecca ran crying upstairs. Behind her closed bedroom door, she removed the pink dress she loved so much. Her fingers trembled as she undid the buttons. Then a pink rose fell from the dress to the floor. The rose had already withered. Just like my happy day, Rebecca thought, tears flooding her cheeks.

Later that same evening Jeremiah Cobb was eating his supper alone at the table by the kitchen window. His wife was nursing a sick neighbor. Rain was falling and the heavens were dark. Looking up, he saw Rebecca at the open door. Her face was so swollen with weeping that he scarcely recognized her.

"Mr. Cobb," began Rebecca in a shaky voice, "I've run away and I want to go back to the farm."

She leaned her head against Mr. Cobb's shoulder and told him about her troubles with Aunt Miranda.

Mr. Cobb said, "I suppose your mother will be real glad to see you back again?"

"She won't like it that I ran away, but I'll make her understand. I'll ask my older sister to come here in my place. The aunts wanted her instead of me, anyway."

"I think your mother sent you here to get some schooling. But you can get that in Temperance, I suppose?"

"There are only two months of school in Temperance, and the farm's too far from all the other schools."

"Oh, well, there are other things besides education," responded Mr. Cobb, slicing two pieces of apple pie.

"How is the school down here in Riverboro—pretty good?"

"Oh, it's a splendid school! And Miss Dearborn is a splendid teacher!"

"Well, my wife met Miss Dearborn on the bridge and asked her, 'How's the little Temperance girl getting along?' and Miss Dearborn said, 'Oh, she's the best I have! I could teach school from sunup to sundown if my students were all like Rebecca Randall.'"

"Oh, Mr. Cobb, *did* she say that?" Rebecca suddenly glowed, her face sparkling. "I'll study the covers right off of the books now."

"You would if you stayed. Now isn't it too bad you've got to give it all up on account of your aunt Miranda? Well, I can't hardly blame you. She's cranky and she's sour, and I guess you aren't much on patience, are you?"

"Not very much."

"Jane'll be real sorry tomorrow to find you've gone away, I guess. But it can't be helped. My wife was talking with her after church the other night. 'You wouldn't know the brick house,' said Jane. 'I'm teaching a sewing school now. What do you think of that? And I'm going to the Sunday school picnic with Rebecca.' My missis said she has never seen Jane look so young and happy."

Mr. Cobb and Rebecca looked at each other in silence. Rebecca, however, could hear her heart pounding. Outside, the rain tapered off, then stopped. A rosy light now filled the room. Through the window, she could see a beautiful rainbow arching like a bridge across the sky.

Rebecca suddenly realized bridges were meant to help people cross difficult places. Mr. Cobb seemed to have built a bridge over her troubles and given her strength to walk across it. At that moment, she decided to stay and somehow to win Aunt Miranda's approval.

Clad in her best pink dress, Rebecca was off to take tea with the Cobbs one beautiful afternoon. While crossing the bridge to their home, she was overcome by the beauty of the river and leaned over the rail to gaze at the dashing torrent of the waterfall. She stood there dreaming until she realized that the bridge was newly painted. Paint was all over her best dress!

With tears streaming from her eyes, Rebecca ran to the Cobbs, hoping for sympathy and some help. Mrs. Cobb quickly dipped the dress in turpentine while Mr. Cobb offered Rebecca some biscuits.

As he passed the honey, Mr. Cobb said, "Seeing there are fresh paint signs hanging all over the bridge, I can't quite figure how you got into the pesky stuff."

"I didn't notice the signs," Rebecca said regretfully.

By the time she was ready to leave, the frock was dry. But the colors had faded with the rubbing, the pattern was blurred, and muddy streaks ran down its front. Rebecca gave the dress one look, put it on, and fled. "If I've got to have a scolding, I want to get it over with quickly."

"Poor little thing!" whispered Mr. Cobb as his eyes followed her down the hill. "I wish she would pay some attention to the ground under her feet. But if she were our child, I'd let her slop paint all over the house before I would scold her the way Miranda does!"

At the brick house, Rebecca took her scolding like a soldier. Among the things Aunt Miranda said to Rebecca was that a child so absent-minded was sure to grow up into a driveling fool. Rebecca did not wish to grow into a fool of any sort, let alone a driveling one. So, to give herself discipline, she decided to punish herself every time Aunt Miranda was displeased with her.

But how? She would make a sacrifice—*give up* something! Yes, that would do it!

She looked about the room at her meager possessions. Yes, the beloved pink parasol! She would throw the frivolous thing into the well. She made her way out the front door, lifted the cover of the well, shuddered, and flung the parasol down.

Next morning, however, a workman had trouble drawing water from the well. He lifted the cover, looked down closely, and managed to remove the parasol. Its ivory handle had jammed the well's chain gear.

Rebecca explained to Aunt Miranda—or tried to—that she had sacrificed her parasol to make up for her faults. But her aunt said, "Now see here, Rebecca, you're too big to be whipped. Next time you think you haven't been punished enough, just tell me and I'll invent a little something more for you!"

The Simpson family was very poor, and the children often went hungry. Their father was still in jail as Thanksgiving approached. Soon everyone else would be feasting on plump turkeys and golden pumpkin pies. They, however, would be forced to beg for scraps outside neighbors' kitchen doors—something they had done many times before.

The children had almost given up hope completely when one of them heard about the Excelsior Soap Company. It offered a prize to any of its young agents who could sell a certain amount of soap door-to-door. And that's exactly what the Simpson children decided to do. They weren't interested in the small amount of money being offered as the prize—they wanted the banquet lamp. To them, it was more desirable than a banquet itself.

The Simpson children would have to sell three hundred cakes of Snow-White and Rose-Red Soap in order to earn this polished brass wonder with the crinkled crepe-paper shade. They asked Rebecca to help—and, of course, she said she would. With the aunts away for a weekend, Rebecca was allowed to stay over at Emma Jane Perkins's house. It was a perfect opportunity for the two of them to work together.

Emma Jane and Rebecca loaded several large boxes of the soap onto the back of Mr. Perkins's wagon. Then the two girls drove along the country road. At the gate of each house, Rebecca held the horse while Emma Jane took the soap samples and knocked at the door. After an hour, she had sold only a few bars. Both girls were getting a little discouraged.

Now it was Rebecca's turn. On the porch of a house, sitting in a rocking chair, was a good-looking young man husking corn. He had a smooth face and a well-trimmed mustache, and wore well-fitting clothes. Rebecca asked, "Is the lady of the house at home?"

"I am the lady of the house at present," answered the man with a whimsical smile. "What can I do for you?"

"Have you ever heard of—would you like—I mean, do you need any soap?" stammered Rebecca.

"Do I look unwashed?"

Rebecca laughed. "I didn't mean *that*! I have some soap to sell. I mean, I would like to introduce to you a very remarkable soap, the best on the market. It is called the —"

"Oh, I know that soap," interrupted the smiling gentleman. "Made out of pure vegetable fats, isn't it?"

"The very purest!" agreed Rebecca.

"No acid in it?"

"Not a trace!" What luck, thought Rebecca, to find a customer who knew all the virtues of the soap. She smiled

more and more. And at her new friend's invitation, she sat down on a porch stool. Rebecca showed him the fine ornamental box that held the soap.

"I'm just visiting my aunt. She's out on a visit herself right now," explained the gentleman. "I used to live in this house as a boy. I'm very fond of it."

"I don't think anything can take the place of a farm. I used to live on one when I was a child." Rebecca sounded like someone well beyond her years.

The man looked at her and put down his ear of corn. "So you consider your childhood a thing of the past, do you, young lady?"

"I can still remember it," answered Rebecca gravely, "though it seems a long time ago."

"I can remember mine, and a particularly unpleasant one it was," said the stranger.

"So was mine," sighed Rebecca. "What was your worst trouble?"

"Lack of food and clothes, mostly."

"Oh!" exclaimed Rebecca sympathetically. "Mine was no shoes and too many babies and not enough books. But you're all right and happy now, aren't you?"

"I'm doing pretty well," said the man. "Now tell me, what are you going to do with the magnificent profits from this business?"

"We are not selling for our own benefit," Rebecca confided. "My friend who is holding the horse at the gate is the daughter of a rich blacksmith and doesn't need any money. I am poor, but I live with my aunts in a brick house. Of course, they wouldn't like me to be a peddler. We are trying to win a wonderful prize for some friends of ours."

And before she knew it, she was telling the gentleman all about the Simpson family: their poverty, their joyless life, and their need for a banquet lamp to brighten their existence.

"I know what it's like to be without a banquet lamp," laughed the man. "Well, then, I'll take three hundred cakes of soap. That should give it to them, shade and all."

Rebecca's stool was very near to the edge of the porch. At this unexpected offer, she tipped over and fell back into a clump of lilac bushes. The amused young man helped her regain her feet.

"Are you sure you can afford it?" gasped Rebecca.

"If I can't, I'll save on something else."

"What if your aunt doesn't like this kind of soap?"

"My aunt always likes what I like."

"Mine doesn't!"

"Then there's something wrong with your aunt!"

"Or with me!" sighed Rebecca.

"What is your name, young lady?"

"Rebecca Rowena Randall, sir."

"Do you want to hear my name?"

"I know already. I'm sure you must be Mr. Aladdin from the *Arabian Nights* story."

He chuckled. "That's close enough." They walked together to the front gate where "Mr. Aladdin" removed all their cartons of soap from the back of the wagon. Then he tucked

the old lap robe cozily over their feet as he said, "Good-bye, Miss Rebecca Rowena Randall!" He said her name as if it gave him great pleasure. "Just let me know whenever you have anything to sell."

"Good-bye, Mr. Aladdin! I surely will!" cried Rebecca, tossing back her hair delightedly and waving her hand.

"Oh, Rebecca!" said Emma Jane in an awestruck whisper. "He raised his hat to us—just like we were real ladies! It'll be *years* before we are."

"Never mind," answered Rebecca. "We are the *beginnings* of ladies—even now."

"He tucked the lap robe around us too," continued Emma Jane. "Oh, isn't he perfectly elegant? What's his name?"

"I don't really know. But I called him Mr. Aladdin because, you see, he gave us a lamp!"

And the lamp did arrive on Thanksgiving. That night, it brightened the Simpsons' house as it had never been brightened before.

A week later, on a chilly winter day, both aunts became ill with colds. Though they tried to do their normal duties, it seemed that the house might slip into disorder.

The next morning, Rebecca awoke before six o'clock. She put on a robe and slippers and tiptoed down the forbidden front stairs. She carefully closed the kitchen door behind her so that no noise could waken the sisters. Then she busied herself for half an hour with early-morning chores. Afterward, she returned to her room to dress.

Aunt Jane had grown worse during the night and couldn't get out of bed. She had both a fever and a headache, and she wondered if her sister could manage without her. Miranda grumbled as she climbed out of bed and splashed water on her face. She blamed everybody she could think of for everything she had to face that day.

Miranda walked through the dining room, then opened the kitchen door. She couldn't believe her eyes and wondered whether she had strayed into the wrong house by mistake.

There was a roaring fire in the stove. The teakettle was singing as it sent out a cloud of steam. Pushed over its spout was a note with "Compliments of Rebecca" scrawled on it. The coffeepot was perking, and cold potatoes and corned beef were on a tray. Another note that said "Regards from Rebecca" was stuck on the chopping knife. Loaves of bread were ready for toasting, the doughnuts were set out, the milk was skimmed, and the butter had been brought in from the dairy.

Miranda sank into the kitchen rocker, muttering under her breath, "She is the most amazing child! I declare, she's all Sawyer!"

The shock of what she saw did not change Miranda completely, however. Her character and thinking had hardened over many years. It wasn't likely that a nice breakfast would undo all that. Still, Miranda *did* become less

harsh in her judgments of Rebecca after that day. The aunt
came to believe that Rebecca had received her goodness from
Sawyer ancestors, *her* side of the family and from Miranda's
direct influence. Everything that was interesting in Rebecca
and every display of ability or talent were soon credited by
Miranda to the brick house training she had given the child.
It made Miranda feel proud. She was convinced she had
made a success out of the least promising material—Rebecca.
But not once did Miranda ever show Rebecca that pride or
any affection either.

The next years were not easy ones for Rebecca. She went to high school at Wareham and did very well there. But on the day of her graduation, Aunt Miranda suffered a stroke that paralyzed her. Instead of taking a teaching position offered to her, Rebecca returned to the brick house to care for her aunt. Troubles came double for Rebecca when her mother had a bad accident. And so Rebecca went back to Sunnybrook Farm!

Two months passed, two months of steady work — of cooking, washing, ironing, mending, and caring for the children. Rebecca worked hard, never complaining. Then, one day, she received a letter saying that her teaching position had been filled. Rebecca now felt trapped. She longed for the freedom of the big world outside.

Her mother felt it too and cried, "I can't bear it! Here I lie confined to this bed, interfering with everything you want to do. It's all wasted! All my saving and doing without; all your hard study; all Miranda's effort; everything that we thought was going to be the making of your career!"

Rebecca said, "Mother, don't talk so, don't think so!" She sat near the bed. "Don't go and think my time is all over before it's even begun. The old maple tree that's a hundred years old had new leaves this summer, so there must be hope for me at seventeen!"

"You can pretend to be brave," sobbed Aurelia, "but you can't fool me. You've lost your chance at a good job, and because of me you're nothing but a drudge!"

"I may look like a drudge, dressed in a calico apron with flour on my nose," said Rebecca, with laughing eyes. "But this is only a disguise. I really am a princess, and soon I'll claim my kingdom."

Aurelia smiled in spite of her own fears. "I only hope you won't have to wait too long, Rebecca." Aurelia's heart felt as if it would break for her daughter.

Rebecca rose to her feet and looked out the window at the trees. "Mother, there's a postman coming with a letter. It must be from the brick house."

It *was* a letter from the brick house, a letter from Aunt Jane. It said Miranda had died.

Rebecca burst into tears. "Poor, poor Aunt Miranda! She is gone and I couldn't say good-bye to her!"

"You must put on your black dress and go this very instant," said her mother. "Your aunts have done everything in the world for you, and it is your turn to show your thanks. I wish I was able to go to my sister's funeral and prove that I've forgotten and forgiven all she said when I was married.

42

Miranda's acts were softer than her words, and she's made up to you for all she blamed me and your father for."

Aurelia stopped for a moment, her thoughts floating back to the past. "Oh, Rebecca," she continued in a quivering voice, "I remember when Miranda and I were little girls and she took such pride in curling my hair. Another time, when we were grown up, she lent me her best blue muslin dress for the Christmas dance. That was where your father and I met. He asked me to lead the grand march with him. Only afterward did I find out that Miranda thought he'd intended to ask *her*!"

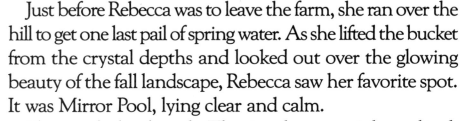

Just before Rebecca was to leave the farm, she ran over the hill to get one last pail of spring water. As she lifted the bucket from the crystal depths and looked out over the glowing beauty of the fall landscape, Rebecca saw her favorite spot. It was Mirror Pool, lying clear and calm.

She caught her breath. The time has come! she realized. I am saying good-bye to Sunnybrook, and the golden gates will close forever now. Good-bye, dear brook and hills and meadows.

Then Rebecca went to wait for the stagecoach. When it pulled up in front of her, a familiar face smiled down at her. It was Mr. Jeremiah Cobb. And once again, he drove her to the brick house. As she rode on top with Mr. Cobb, she recalled the day—seemingly so long ago—when she sat on the box seat for the first time. Her legs dangled in the air, too short to reach the footboard. So much had happened since then! So many friends she had met, including Mr. Adam Ladd, whom she had named Mr. Aladdin. He seemed to be patiently waiting for her to grow up.

Suddenly, the brick house came into view. At the rumble of the approaching stagecoach, the door of the house opened. Aunt Jane, frail and white, came down the stone steps. Rebecca held out her arms and the old aunt slipped into them feebly. Warmth and strength and life flowed from the young woman to the older one.

"Rebecca," said the aunt, raising her head, "before you go in to look at Miranda, do you feel any bitterness over anything she ever said to you?"

"No, Aunt Jane. If anything, I feel gratitude."

"It's true she had a quick temper and a sharp tongue," said Aunt Jane. "But she wanted to do right, and she did it as near as she could. She never said so, but I'm sure she was sorry for every harsh word she spoke to you."

"I told her before I left that she made me what I am," said Rebecca tearfully.

"She didn't do that. You did it yourself. But Miranda did give you some help, I think, and you should be grateful for that."

Rebecca nodded and started into the brick house, but Aunt Jane stopped her once more and said, "Now, Rebecca, I must tell you one more thing. Your aunt Miranda has willed all this to you—the brick house, the buildings and the furniture, and the land all around the house."

Rebecca put her hand to her heart. After a moment, she said, "Let me go in alone. I want to thank her. I feel as if I could make her hear and feel and understand!"

Rebecca went into the room where Miranda's body lay. Quietly, she touched Miranda's hand and bowed her head.

Minutes later, Rebecca came out of the front door. She sat in the doorway, just under the overhanging elms. A great calm had come over her. Rebecca gazed out over the land she now owned. The red and gold colors of autumn bathed the countryside. And in the distance, a river flowed softly toward the sea.

It was home, her roof, her garden, her dear trees. And now it would be home for her little family from Sunnybrook. Her mother would come live here and have the companionship of her sister Jane once more. The children would have teachers and playmates.

Rebecca stood up and walked to the edge of the front yard. She closed her eyes and thought about Aunt Miranda's generosity. She also thought about Mr. Adam Ladd and about teaching.

What would the future bring her? Rebecca couldn't say. But it did not bother her. She was finally at peace.